NEIGHBORHOOD BAND

by Jesse Levine

illustrated by Kate Flanagan

Orlando   Boston   Dallas   Chicago   San Diego

Visit *The Learning Site!*

www.harcourtschool.com

My friends and I started a neighborhood band. Since we didn't have any money for new instruments, we created some.

The drums were easy to make. We used tubs, cans, and a large washtub.

Then we grabbed our sticks and imitated rhythms we had heard other bands play. That's how we learned to play rhythm on the drums.

Then we got some old things from our kitchens. We hung these things on a rope and hit them with spoons. They made some great sounds! Now we could play both rhythms and tunes.

4

Diana brought a shoe box and a large
bottle. We put rubber bands around the box.
It became a banjo!

We poured some water into the bottle. It became a flute!

Richard and Joline appeared from around
the corner. "May we play, too?" they asked.
Richard made a horn from a plastic tube.
Joline made a kazoo from a cardboard tube.

We practiced a lot. Choosing the songs to play was sometimes difficult. Playing the songs was more fun!

Our songs had good rhythm and tunes. They were also loud!

We were probably too loud for Mrs. Dix. When we played, she closed her doors and windows. She never asked us to stop playing, though.

One day Mr. Marks startled us when he appeared at his door. He is a train conductor at night and he sleeps during the day. We thought he would say we were too loud, but he began to dance to the music.

"Your band sounds good," he said. "It's loud, but it's good. I like lively music."

That made us feel proud.

Come hear
The Neighborhood Band
perform on
Saturday at 10 A.M. in
the Rodriguez's yard.
Bring a chair or blanket
to sit on.

Then we got an idea. We decided to
perform for our neighborhood. We asked all
our families and neighbors to come and
hear us.

We served cookies and fruit punch as
everyone arrived.

We played a lot of songs, and everyone clapped when we were finished.

The Neighborhood Band was a big success. All summer long we practiced and performed together and had a good time.